I Knew I'd find YOU.

I knew I'd find YOU.

I knew we'd find you, i
knew it would be soon.
You're here by our side
and we're over the moon.
We're thankful each day,
for you we adore.
We love you so much, its
hard to ignore.

This story begins
with some clouds
and two bubbles.
It rained and it
poured, they
wanted no trouble.

The bubbles fell down
and landed in water.
One was a son and
the other a daughter.

The water went round, fast in a spin.

When it had stopped the bubbles could swim.

The bubbles were
named Petrie and Ivy.
Both really tiny but
both just as mighty.

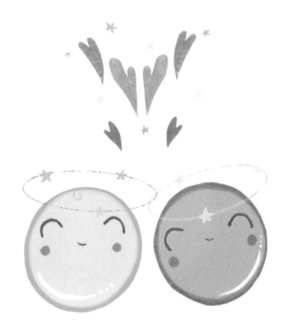

Petrie and Ivy were
very dizzy.
They had each other
they weren't in a tizzy.

Under the water, swam
past a shoal.
They left someone behind,
it was two sad tadpoles.

"Don't be sad" said Ivy.
"you can come with us, you
can climb inside me."

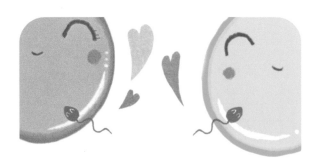

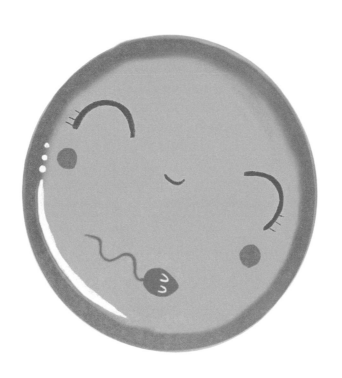

Feeling brave they went to
explore.
They were not afraid or
scared anymore.
Bubbles and tadpoles began
to feel lost. All of a sudden,
an icy cold frost.

The frost froze the
bubbles still. They
could not move, they
started to chill.

A bright light shone, and out came the sun. Having one bubble is better than none.

Ivy felt
warm and
began to
thaw.
The only bad
thing, they
were
together no
more.

Ivy missed Petrie but she wasn't too sad, the tadpole inside her made her feel glad. Being alone and so far apart, inside of Ivy was a beat of a heart.

Washed up on an
island, all squishy
and new. Ivy
shouted to Petrie...

"I will try to find you!"

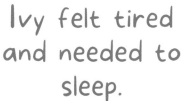

Ivy felt tired
and needed to
sleep.
The sleep that
she had was
ever so deep.

The tadpole inside
her began to grow.

What will it be?
We did not know.

Arms and legs started to show.

Ivy and tadpole together they grew.
Into a baby! Oh wow! Who knew!
Baby Ivy was a dream come true.
Worth the wait, she was long overdue.

Ivy did not forget
about Petrie.
Where on earth
could he be?
How will she find
him, he's smaller
than a pea.

Petrie found
the island, he
washed up on
shore.
He had a
funny feeling
Ivy's been here
before.

He dug a big
hole right down
to the core.
He fell asleep
inside it and
started to
snore.

Z
 Z
Z

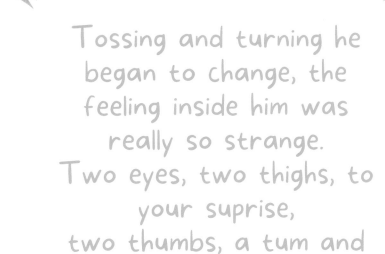

Tossing and turning he
began to change, the
feeling inside him was
really so strange.
Two eyes, two thighs, to
your suprise,
two thumbs, a tum and
even a bum.
Hips, lips and finger tips.

Until the day
another baby was
born.
Out he popped like

POPPING
POPCORN!

His Mummy and Daddy and
someone he knew.
He wasn't too sure, he
needed a clue.
His sister Ivy, could it be
true?
She whispered to him...

"I knew I'd find you."

It means dear baby, you
will always be treasured.
Our love for you can not
be measured.
We hoped and prayed our
dream would come true,
Our world is complete now
that we have found you.

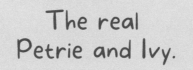

The real
Petrie and Ivy.

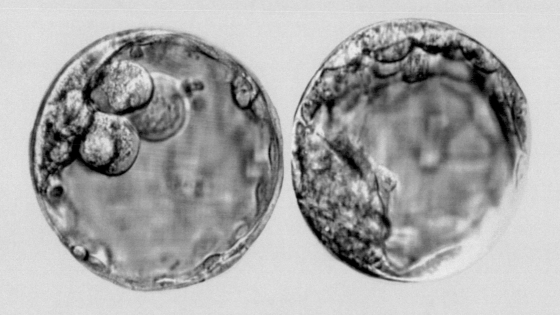

My name is Stacey Morgan, I am the writer
and illustrator of this story. A short while
ago my husband and I started our IVF
journey. I had **2** eggs collected. I dreamt and
thought about our embryos constantly, will
they survive? What is happening to them?
What stage are they at now?
So I channeled that anxiety and worry into
a writing a story for them. This was how
my book 'I knew I'd find you' came to life.

Our **2** embryos became Petrie (Petri dish)
and Ivy (IVF) and their great big adventure
is the stages of IVF from an egg to baby.
Portrayed in the imaginative way, not the
clinical way. It's a heart warming, feel good
story suitable for all children but especially
if you have a miracle IVF baby!

I dreamt of a story and made it into reality in a book. I dream of being a mother so hopefully one day that dream will become reality too. Anything that consumes your dreams is powerful, right?

I hope my story will encourage others to stay strong and not to give up hope on their dreams.

My book was written for the ones that never came to be. Gone but not forgotten, now they will always be with me.

If you liked this book, check out the Authors others on Amazon

Made in United States
Troutdale, OR
02/18/2024